CATHARTICS

ILLUSTRATED & WRITTEN

BY

JOESPH N. MUNOZ

TO MY FRIENDS
& FAMILY

2015.

Weeks after the terrible March Sixth. If to ask anybody,

would have different views. Just twenty years earlier of the dreadfull

September eigth attack, that has brought the same trgic instances.

The Hayriders, a band of theives on trucks full of Hay, Caused both these events before.

But never caught.

Draws, Gabe,Katie, Sutton & Jonas finish school. Gabe's god parent,

Paddy. Is to look after everyone. That won't be enough, of the cursed events to take place in

... New Jersey.

3.

Chapter one

May 14th, Garden State Parkway, Old Bridge NJ

" Are you thinking like a fool or not?"

" Look at you " Draws said. " A rock!" - " I'll be a rock when i knock you out! :
I'mma trying to be serious here.. hehe, Stop! - " Me, I'm a little nervous about.. do you think-"

- " Mama Mia! here we go again, Draws has gotta relax Sometimes!" Gabe told Draws.

5.

Draws accidentally forgets to ask permission to clean up the mess from the teacher.

Draws didn't even know what he just did.
Gabe laughs, They forget all about it, Back to Square one. Gabe is serious.

6.

" You know a flying cow can fly when sitting.

Cause the earth rotates all by itself & when a cow jumps, They can fly for one second ".

Draws logic, The way he sounded so genuine to Gabe, Made him angry & laughing.

Draws is serious but it didn't fool Gabe. He already had enough.

But couldn't take it seriously.

Katie " the loose canon " who works harder for a future career.

" ooh Gabe gotta leave Draws alone, Its too crowded in here " Katie said.

" You have a job. The best case scenario you get hired, But than in all doubt,

Not ready for the comitment, The first paycheck & you dash out.

But remeber that everyone has a job. You'll have to grow up. "

Gabe tries to act serious, But always stampled by Drawing's sense of humor.

gotta start getting ready for Halloween, Its that weather again" Katie said,-

Depending on whats going on with the world" Gabe says,

s getting creepy now".

aws leaves his pencil on the table.

Chapter two

Paddy & Sutton are at home. Now everyone is out of school for good at least, for the summer.
Sutton lives like the queen. But there are worse things to be happening than just sitting arund all day.

" In the beging, You knew it was going to happen. Just in the begining of the year,
Talked about going into the navy.

Just to show how serious you are in the new world."

Katie doesn't mind draws. Draws might've not remeebered,

since Katie & Draws were little in the small classes. Katie wasn't in school as much always in & out.

The reason is very intresting, But personal.

10.

Jonas comically expierienced, More social than
Gabe but always trying to find a way out. Jonas can teach
Gabe a thing about being more social than Angry.

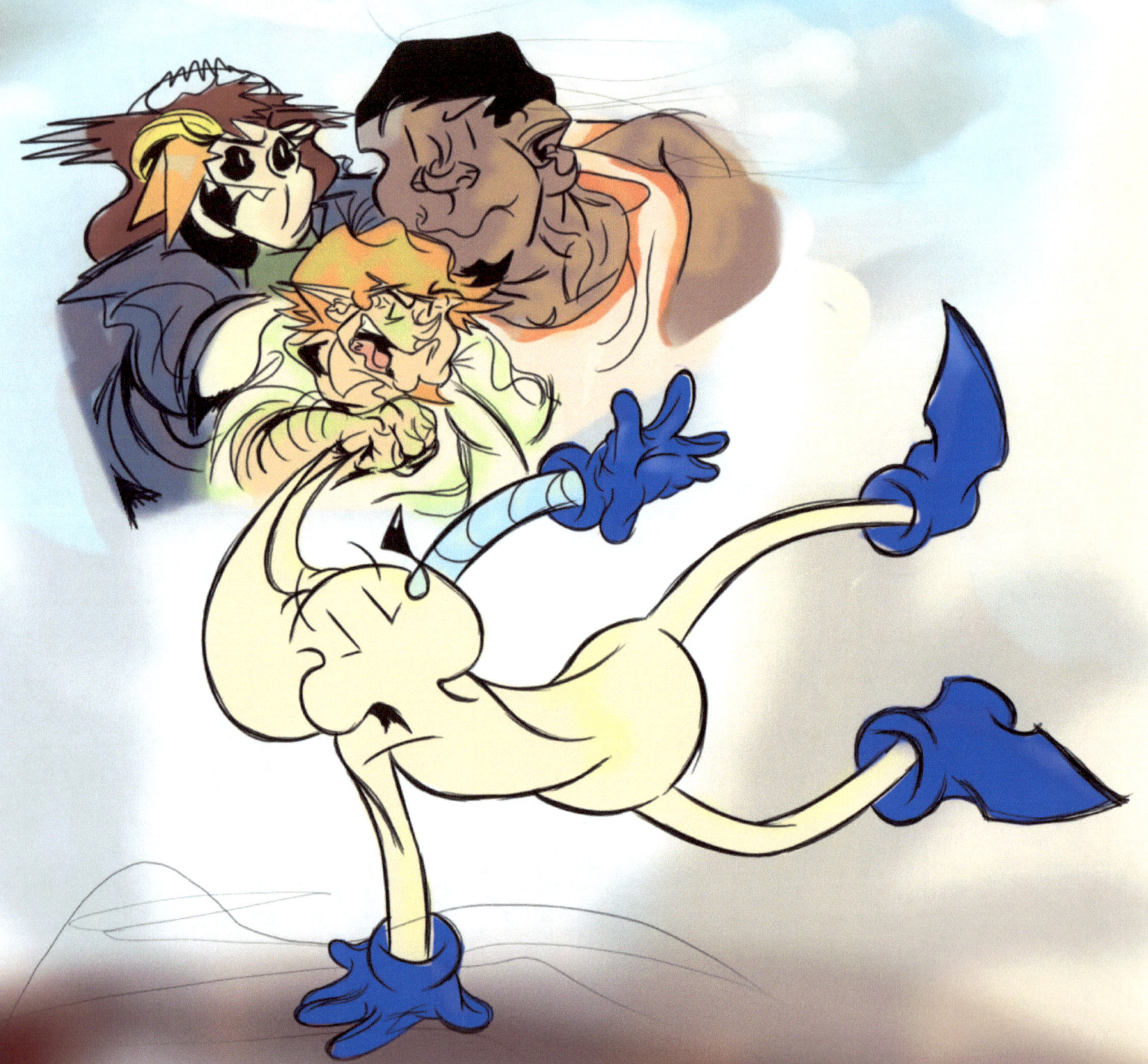

Draws thought
(I'll make the problem as difficult as possible that it might work.)

Sayreville

Paddy want's Jonas number for Decoration advice.

Draws asks if Paddy wants any of his paintings & his number.

Paddy doesn't need Draw's number.

Chapter three

Paddy grew up in Sunnyside Queens, NYC .

Moved down to New Jersey. Gabe after he came back from spenidng his tweens in Italy & Became his god parent.

Sutton, Gabe's sister makes fun of Draws. Paddy knowing the most important thing to make sure of his summer plans.

" Katie went some where elsethat i couldn't find her, Just like my sister. The story of my life." Gabe said. " Shes like my cousin"

Jonas looked as if he was smiling throgh the awkwardness, within the minute, he almost cried. The pressure of being the " Excorcist" can be very alarming.

" Paddy, where were u on September eigth?"

- " I don't like to talk about september eigth"!

n thinking of what happened to us last month, What was it the same with us than it was with you, like twenty years ago?" Draws asks.

" Good question is it easier if i told you where were you on March sixth?"

" We don't really like to talk about March sixth"

- " AH! So you see it's easier for me because you can say i already lived through something like this before,

So the second time should be much easier!?"

- " ....Ok, i understand."

May 17th

" Through out these days, feels like floating after you think after you think about it. But back than in reality felt stuck,

Than you realise its Friday instead of Monday."

In the morning Draws, Gabe, Katie, Sutton, Paddy almost get into an accident on " The cursed Dark road",

To come is the danger ahead. Katie looked back & didn't want to drive again.

15.

Paddy Helped Katie with a bit of help to calm down. That left Drawing's to drive.
Waiting in the car. Paddy & Jonas argue with each other.
" Ooowoo look at chu', Interseting !" - " I can argue about this all day long, . I'm having fun" Paddy loves to mimmick Jonas with a smile.
" You put the fridge in the attic yet?" - " Here we go again" Sutton sighs.
" Theres no! Fridge in the attic !" - "nonono, He didn't put the fridge in the attic yet, Pat."
16.

The only wise guy, Paddy was fooling was himself. He was dumb founded on how his " Kids". That they worked so hard. He remebered to look both ways before crossing the street.

Like another person was living inside of him. His " common-sense" or another personality.

17.

Draws accidentally rear ends somebody's car.
Draws parks the car all the way in the back of the parking lot.

Everyone must now walk now... He didn't realize he'd park so far.

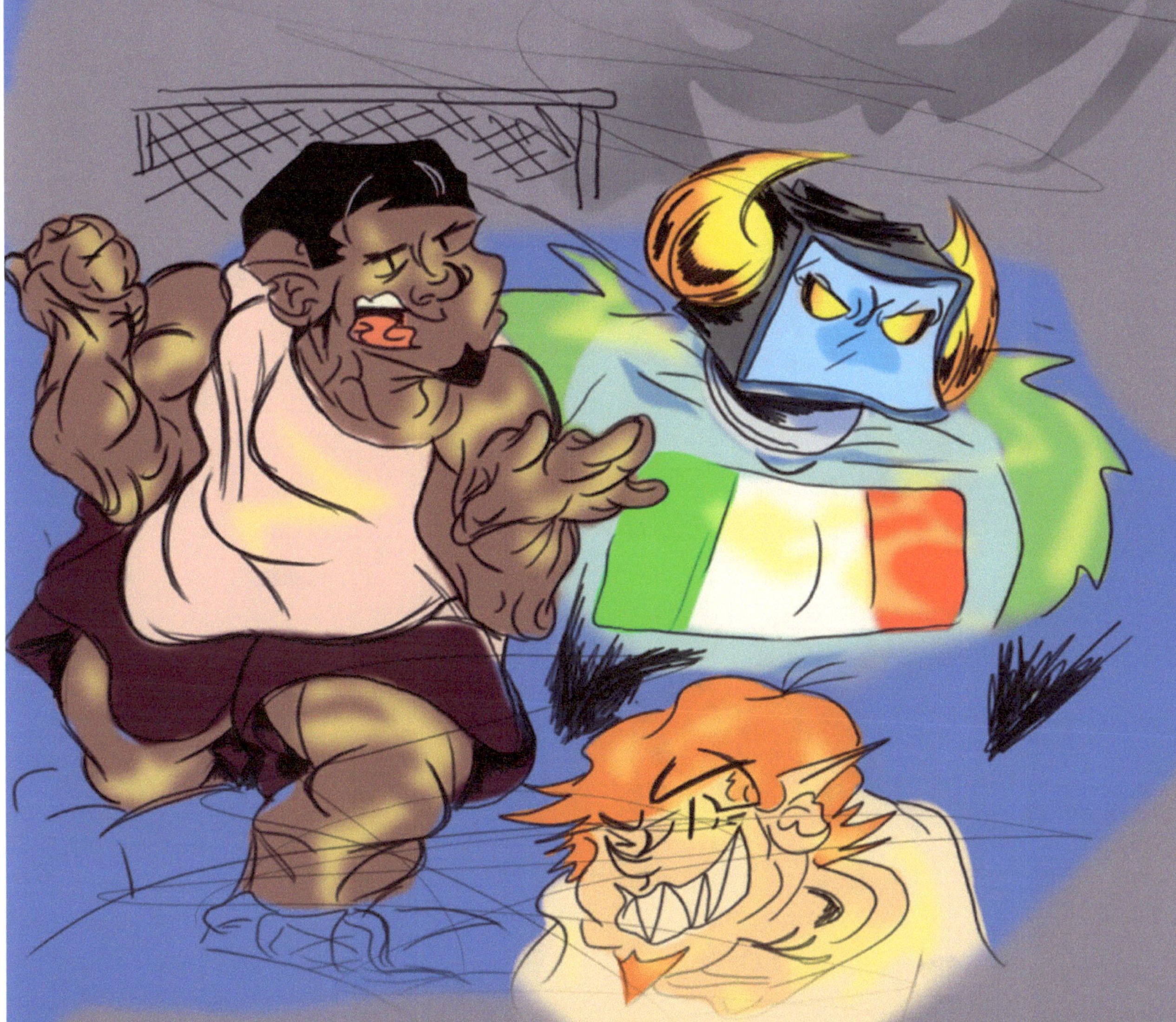

**" To think that everybody had to be studying & working hard,
But the opposite is true."**

Point Pleasent

18.

A group of strangers, Talking about One-billion lives right next to a dinosaur display.

Gabe's other friends show up & talk about soccer. But later on they get into trouble with the poli

With a problem with a bike.

" Draws, don't tell Paddy about what happened.

Or else cause it just got crazy". Gabe said, " You said it." Draws noticed.

Katie meetsa a creepy stranger in a line.

Katie in line, looking in front of somebody.
The person in front looks behind Katie,
For a real long time. A scared look.

Katie looks to the side of the stranger until she looks behind her.
When the person in front of Katie turns to where Katie is looking,
Katie dashes, turns & walks. Katie examing the problem.

21.

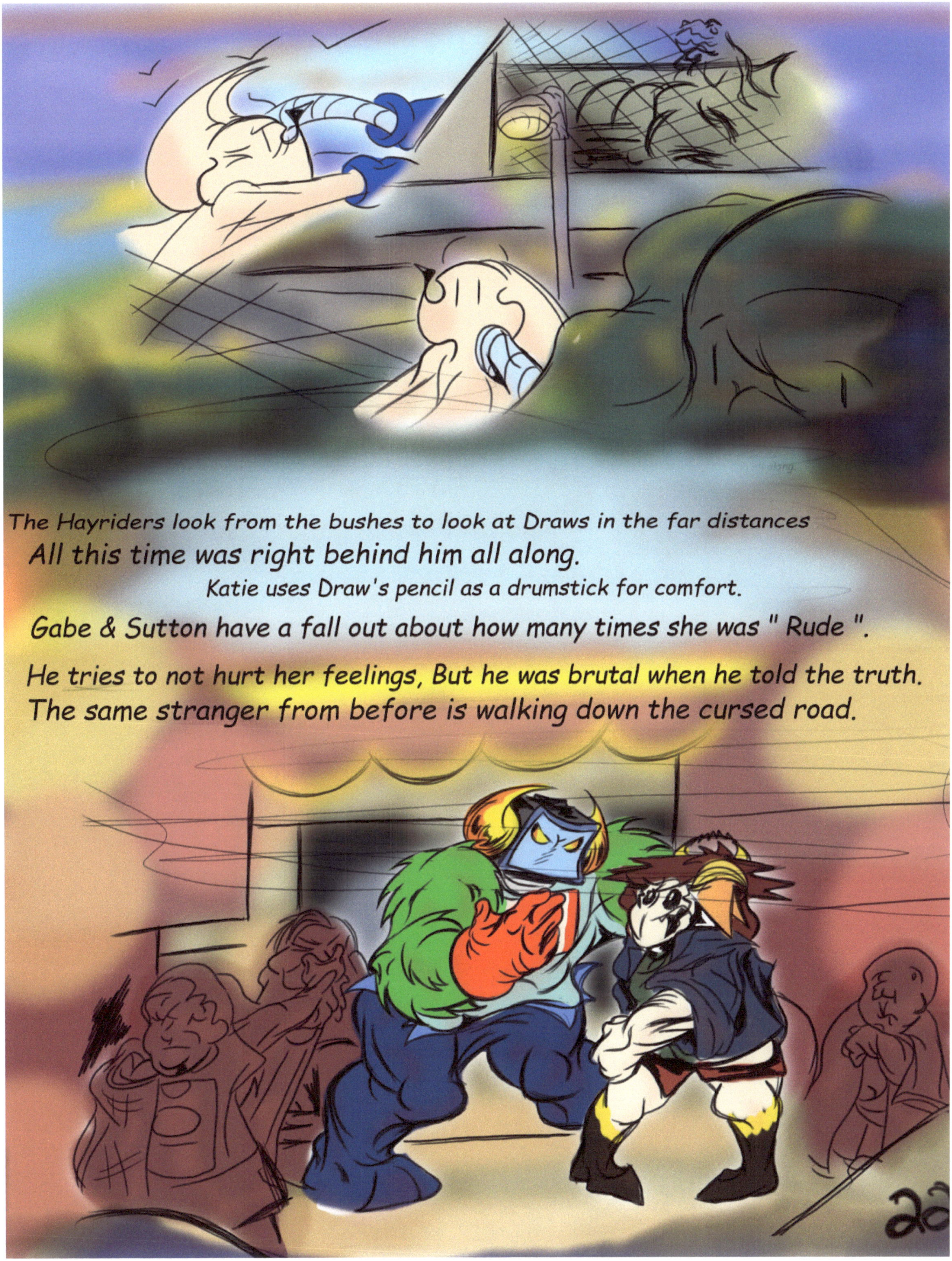

The Hayriders look from the bushes to look at Draws in the far distances
All this time was right behind him all along.
Katie uses Draw's pencil as a drumstick for comfort.
Gabe & Sutton have a fall out about how many times she was " Rude ".
He tries to not hurt her feelings, But he was brutal when he told the truth.
The same stranger from before is walking down the cursed road.

23.

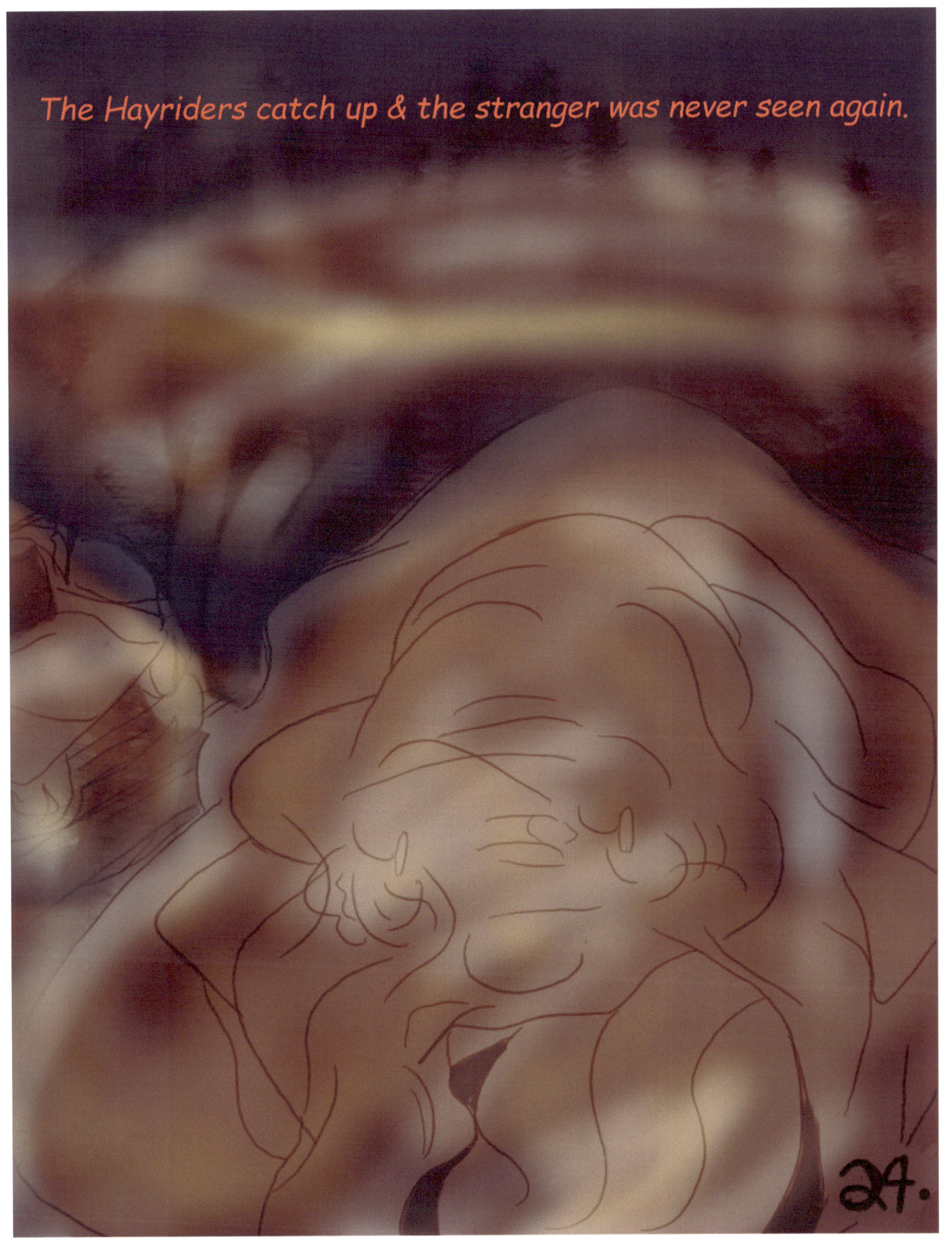
The Hayriders catch up & the stranger was never seen again.
24.

25.

26.

27.

28.

Chapter Four

May 21rst

Draws gets bullied " DId you just come from dumb city?!"

Gabe looks in a store for more jewlery.

Katie practices cutting hair with her scissors.

Katie loved her friend,

She was happy & sad at the same time for her
friend that did a great job.

Draws was astonished.

29.

Katie still rembered growing up in Brooklyn
for the little time she spent, She loved the city.

Jonas is thrilled to see what jewlery Gabe sells.

Jonas loved to play basketball on the street.

That he had from when he was in Maimi,

where he heard strange voices in the sky.

30.

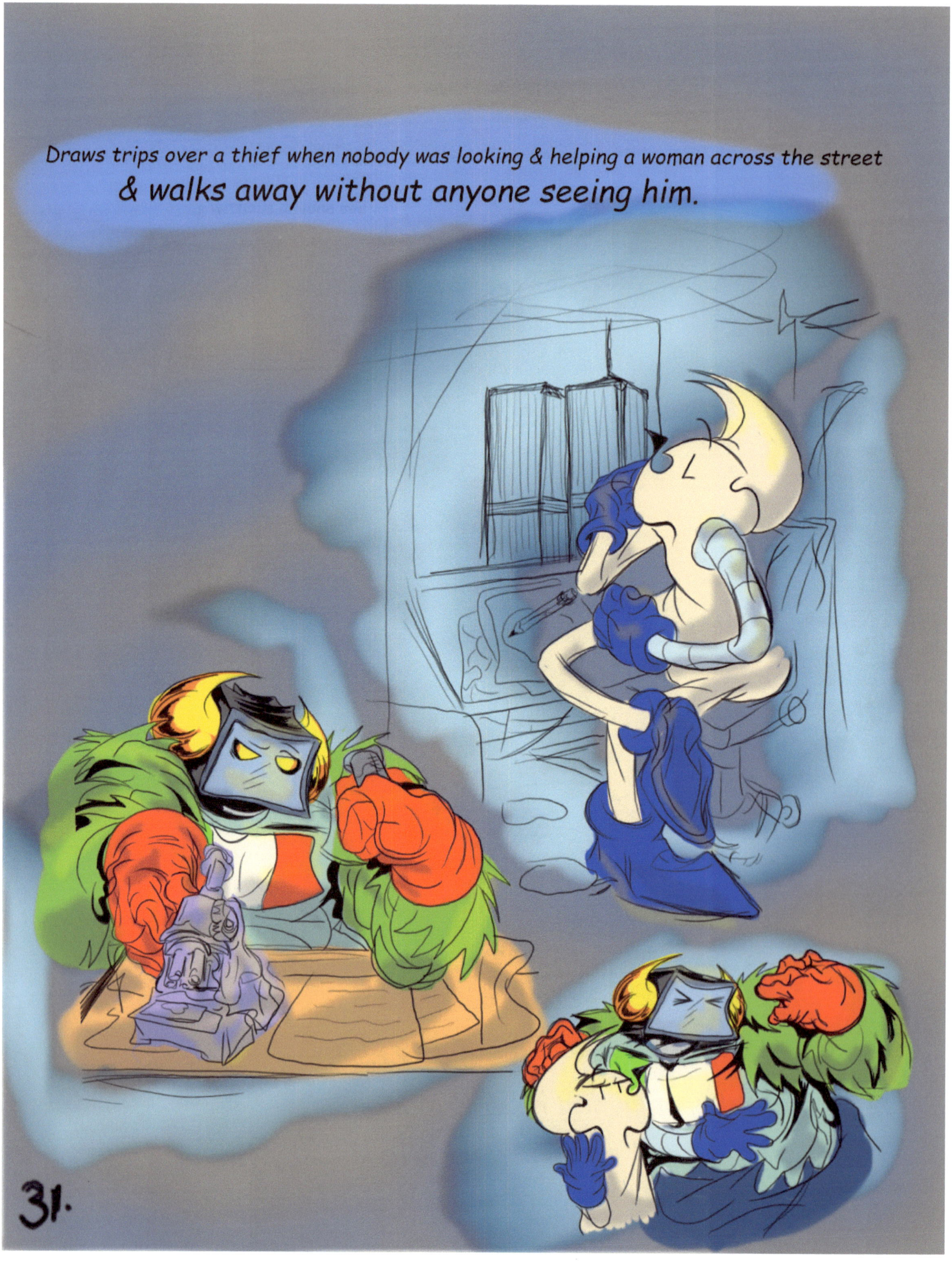

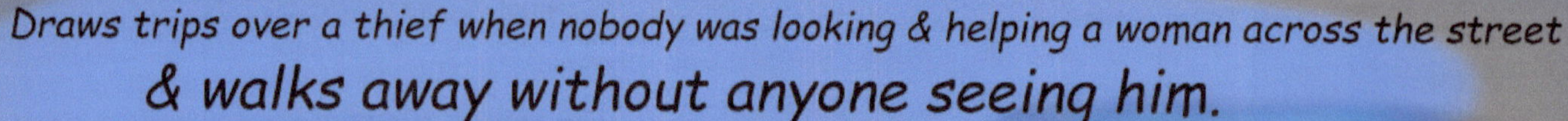

Draws trips over a thief when nobody was looking & helping a woman across the street
& walks away without anyone seeing him.

31.

Sutton prepared to head out for the day, By annoying Paddy. Having to drive her to the gym.
Gabe had to drive her instead. Sutton knew that her brother Gabe was working like an animal,
" Poor guy was killin' himself."
32.

Chapter five

Gabe pictured himself in a place somewhere else, Peaceful, To get his mind straight like the beach.

Draws wanted to be an Artist, Gabe wanted to be a doctor.

" Omigod! he really did a number on me, You won't believe what he did!" Gabe said -" What"-

" He tricked me for a whole year, He made me think he was twenty!" -"Pfft, Omigod " Katie laughed. Katie was a major in psycho

The stranger from when Katie was in line. Panicked! Katie understandably wierded out,

But she was scared, But the person had gotte'em in the problem in the first place,

Katie felt devastated & worried.

To pass the same curse to another.

Paddy uses Katie's scissors to cut sheets of napkins. " To be senseless. But the world is great."

" yeah, I bet a bunch of good lookin' mamas! must've been there." Paddy was intersested.

- " yeah it was great" Draws was in another world. -" Glad there was no trouble"

- " Yeah, nono - I mean there was this thing with the friend than they brought out the dogs- tha-'

' - " Omigod!, I'mma kick yo butt". Gabe shouted at draws.

Gabe is much bigger than Draws, Gabe asks questions Draws should be asking.

Paddy with his shoe collection " Don't forget to put a tv in the fridge in the attic!"

Gabe was like playfully laughing " You knew, you made a mistake, who do you think you fooli

Gabe had enough because sometimes it can be out of this world.

33.

34.

" You want to see certain things you gotta do with your friends,

But they say " But you gotta go to school" Just shows how much your friends are your friends

" Why didn't i think of that " Draws says.

" Everybody is having a good time because of how,
through out everything was funny & beutiful all it was just to ask is to not do one stupid thing."

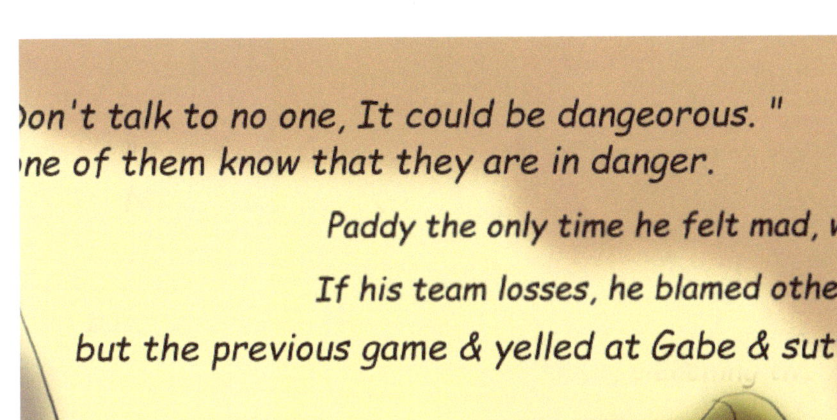

Don't talk to no one, It could be dangeorous. "
ne of them know that they are in danger.

Paddy the only time he felt mad, was at a baseball game.

If his team losses, he blamed others not because of the present game,
but the previous game & yelled at Gabe & sutton playfully.

Katie goes towards the door,

clenching the knob not getting through the door..

Not knowing that the Hayriders are right behind the door.

36.

Chapter six

Chaos Erupts, spine chilling with watery eyes in shock.
Draws meets the Hayriders, Gabe takes an instant dislike to the Hayriders.

37.

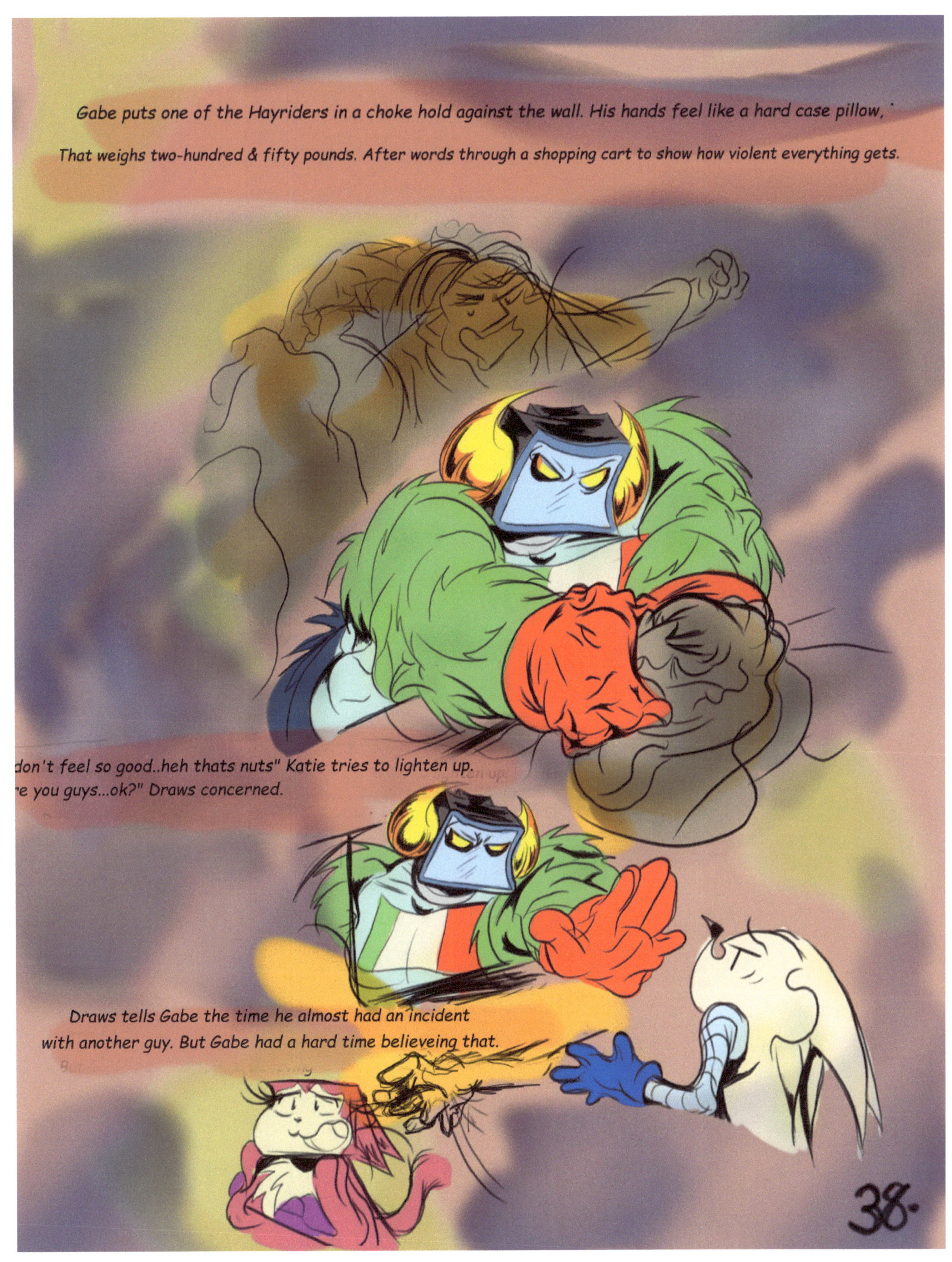
Gabe puts one of the Hayriders in a choke hold against the wall. His hands feel like a hard case pillow,
That weighs two-hundred & fifty pounds. After words through a shopping cart to show how violent everything gets.
don't feel so good..heh thats nuts" Katie tries to lighten up.
re you guys...ok?" Draws concerned.
Draws tells Gabe the time he almost had an incident
with another guy. But Gabe had a hard time believeing that.
38.

Draws grabbed the Hayriders & got so mad that the room went silent.

Even Gabe was shocked & so was Katie.
" That never happened before?.." Katie found intersting.

" After words in an instant. You in the present,
messed up & nobody takes you seriously,
But i't doesn't matter cause " Thats why you gotta go to school, dummy!"

After the shopping cart incident, The Hayriders had come back with the secret weapon,

But a that point Draws, Gabe & Katie were gone at that point.
Meanwhile a kid drops her wallet. Sutton returns it, without anyone knowing. .

Sutton can tell the truth & lie when faceing responsibilities. But the consequences come back later.

Chapter Seven

"Play-one liners, take them by surprise, " didn't think he'd say that".
Making goofs, clumsy, :get your freinds in an accident,
But you're reaaly nervous while driving."

Paddy asks everybody to help him find his missing shoe,
So now it hits everyone that they must go on a quest!

41.

Draws meets the guy who bullied him from before.
-"Dumb city!" - " Yeah! yo mother called she says hi"! Draws yelled.

With school, Sutton got herself into more danger she gets a empty envelope, .
Sets it on fire & almost rips on a frog.

Sutton loves to collect " Kid's meal" collector toys.
Draws gets distracted by Sutton's toys.

They go to the " Dark road".
which they don't know it was the same road from before.

42.

Paddy was carefully & trying to be aware of the surroundings.

Draws finds some dinosaurs, that Sutton thought was lying, But was near scared to death.

Tha Hayriders go out looking for a basketball,

Knowing that One-Billion lives are about to be extinct. According to plan.

43.

Mean while,.. Jonas hosts a town meeting at a church, confronting a panicked town.
44.

Chapter Eight

Jonas calms down a crowd member like " a Priest calming down a demon".
Jonas can be more social with a lot of expierience.

Some one in the crowd brings up
" The dark Road Curse". Jonas goes hand in hand with the Dark road.

Jonas is terrified to never wish his worst enemy to go down the dark road

45.

Jonas is shell shocked, Doesn't know what to say.

" The sun melts the cold, So the cold melts for the sun,

Cause if the sun wasn't there to begin with. It wouldn't melt anything."

Jonas trying to lighten the mood.

46°

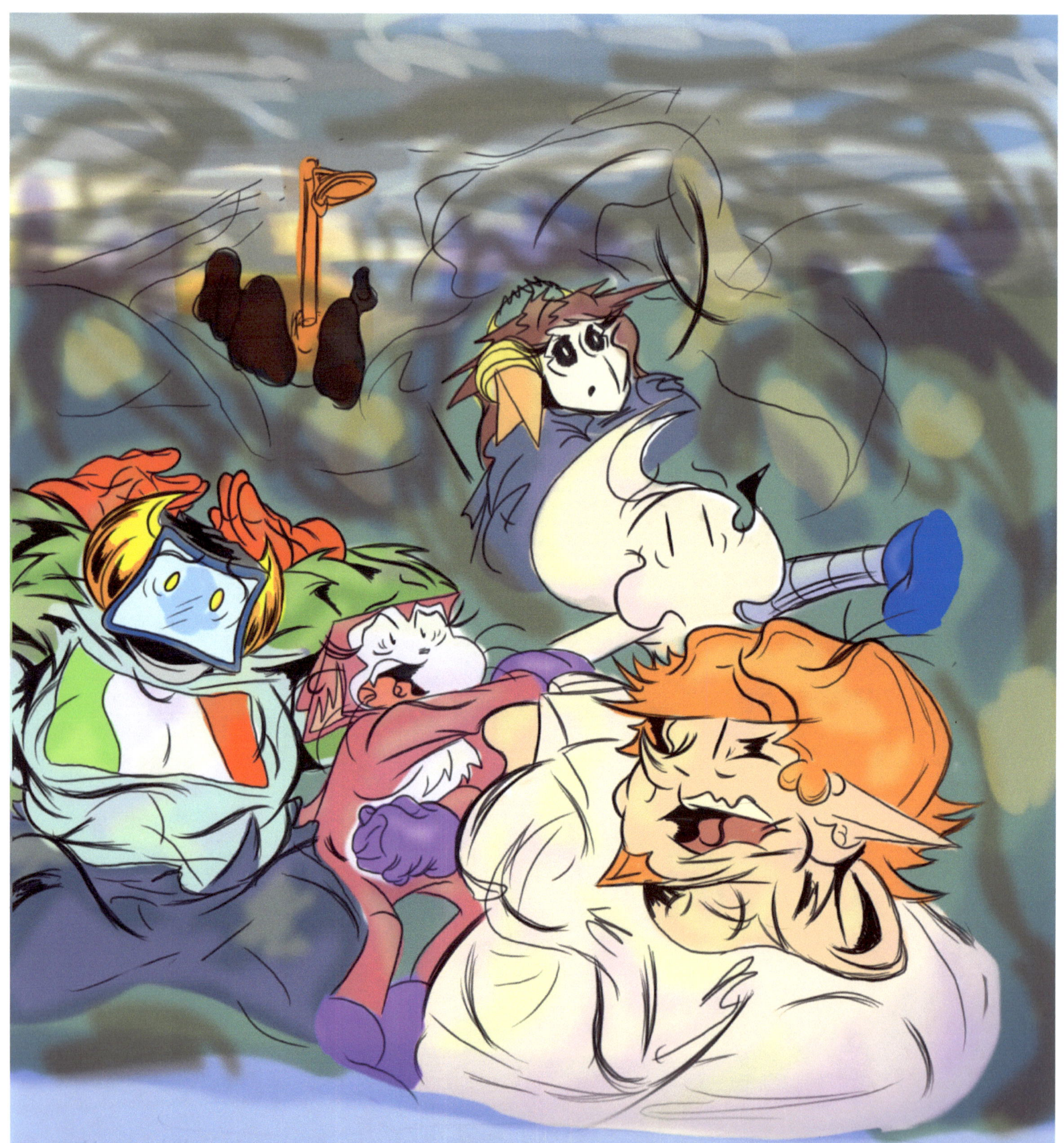

Mean while,.. Paddy always lies.

But he wasn't lying when he thought he saw his old friends

from across the street. Katie tried to warn him but it was too late.

47.

Gabe throws Jonas Basketball, He borrowed.
raws, Gabe, Katie, Sutton & Paddy with little injury with fighting.
The Hayriders disapeared.
48.

" Are you thinking like a fool or not?"
Chapter Nine
May 24th
Neithier does anyone else, except for the Hayriders.
Now they think that those people saved the day,
But what they don't know it was a freak accident.
" I gotta a story to tell Draws, man! That is Unbelievable.
" Katie as she would describe herself as anyone else would. A descent human being.
49

In the end, Nobody knows. Neithier Draws, Gabe, Katie, Jonas, Sutton & Paddy. The Hayriders are shocked on how this could've happened or how this had happened.

Back in town, At the hospital. Draws tells the time when he saw a person getting into van & disappeared ounce. Gabe doesn't believe him.

Draws & Paddy recognzille. Gabe knew things were changing. He wished he can go somewhere more peaceful.

Hayriders knew this was a big deal & that there was hell to pay.

Cause now they think that these guys did it on purpose,
Not knowing it was an accident. ...To Save One-billion lives!
" We still gotta go to school, But we gotta lot ahead of us."
Not the End!
52.

Chapter Ten

Cathartic's Injury stories

Katie- on March 15th.

she can see from a far distance when she broke her tooth on a broken swing. .
In the hospital. She sees a robber running away,

When he got caught she saw the robber have a family. .

She took care of the family.

Paddy, January 21rst,

Fought in the war. Paddy had meet a lot of famous people that lead him to the enemy bas where he defeated the enemy base.

Draws- April 26th uses his intelligence,
when he was in a car crash by after words fixing the mechanics.
Draws had a broken wrist. He was too furious but to scared to show.
Gabe- got lost in a mall- Feburary 4th.
He uses his strength to lift a toy train.
Just as a surprise actually found a lost service dog under it that bit an old mean lady.
In the end got a broken shoulder.
on April 5th, got in trouble with some kindergarten teacher.
fter words went to the store & when she came out found a toy she didn't
& doesn't know how it got there.
But than got her apendix shot.
Jonas- May 1rst.
Was trying to keep the peace at a chaotic scene, like a excorcism.
Jonas to prove that he is more expierienced with that sort of thing.
But almost dies on accasion.
59.